Emily

A Doubleday Book for Young Readers

by
Michael Bedard

pictures by
Barbara Cooney

Emily

A Doubleday Book for Young Readers

Published by Random House Children's Books
a division of Random House, Inc.
New York

Doubleday and the anchor with dolphin colophon are registered trademarks of
Random House, Inc.

Visit us on the Web! www.randomhouse.com/kids
Educators and librarians, for a variety of teaching tools, visit us at
www.randomhouse.com/teachers

Library of Congress Cataloging-in-Publication Data

Bedard, Michael.
Emily / Michael Bedard; illustrated by Barbara Cooney.
p. cm.
SUMMARY: When a mother and child pay a visit to their reclusive neighbor Emily,
who stays in her house writing poems, there is an exchange of special gifts.
ISBN 978-0-385-30697-3 (alk. paper)—
ISBN 978-0-385-90539-8 (lib. bdg. : alk. paper)
1. Dickinson, Emily, 1830–1886—Juvenile Fiction.
[1. Dickinson, Emily, 1830–1886—Fiction. 2. Neighborliness—Fiction.]
I. Cooney, Barbara, 1917–2000. II. Title.
PZ7.B381798Em 1992
[E]—dc20   91-41806

Printed in the United States of America
November 1992

23 22 21 20 19 18 17 16 15 14

Acknowledgments

The author gratefully acknowledges the help of
the staff at the Dickinson Homestead and
the Jones Library in Amherst, Massachusetts, with
special thanks to Carol Birtwistle and Daniel Lombardo.

For much help and encouragement the illustrator thanks
Carol Birtwistle, Curator, Dickinson Homestead, Amherst College;
Melanie Wisner, Houghton Library, Harvard University;
Susan and Dick Todd;
the Pierpont Morgan Library;
the Boston Athenaeum;
Phoebe Porter and Donald Joralemon;
and last, but not least,
Barnaby Porter, Technical Advisor.

The Publisher especially thanks
the Pierpont Morgan Library, New York,
for permission to reproduce a portion
of an original letter from its collection (MA1556)
written by Emily Dickinson to
Martha Dickinson and Sally Jenkins in 1883.

for Kathy
M.B.

with love to dear Talbot
B.C.

here is a woman on our street they call the Myth. She lives with her sister in the yellow house across the road. Her room is the one up on the left at the front. If you stand on tiptoe, you can see it peeping over the high hedge as you pass.

She hasn't left her house in nearly twenty years. If strangers come to call, she runs and hides herself away. Some people say she's crazy.

But to me she's Emily....

We were still new to the house the day the letter dropped through the slot. I heard it whisper to the floor and ran to pick it up. I peeked through the narrow window in the door. There was no one there but winter, all in white.

Mother was in the parlor practicing when I brought the letter in. As she opened it, a little spray of flowers fell onto the keys. I picked them up. They were dry and flat.

"Dear neighbor," she read, "I am feeling like these flowers. Revive me with your music. It would be spring to me."

"Who is it from?" I asked.

"Nobody, dear," she said.

"Now run along and play. You may take those with you, if you like."

And she tucked the note away.

Upstairs, I laid the flowers on my windowsill beside the box of lily bulbs we had brought from home. They had lain in the cellar, cold and dark all winter long. But Father said that we could plant them soon. He said it would help to make this house our own.

Below, the garden slept beneath the snow. I saw footprints leading down our walk, across the road, and up through the hedge of the yellow house.

A stair creaked as I crept back to my room. I sat in bed and looked across the street. The light shone in her room. A shadow moved upon the shade. Did she sometimes sit there watching me?

Father came to tuck me in.

"Did I hear a little mouse upon the stairs?" he said. "What's that you have there?"

I showed him the little bunch of flowers. Some had crumbled onto the sheets.

"So these came with the letter, then? Bluebells. How beautiful they are. But very delicate, my dear."

He set them gently down upon the windowsill and stood looking across the street.

"Why does she never come out?" I asked.

"I don't know, my dear. People say all sorts of things, but no one really knows."

"Sing me the night song," I said.

He knelt down by the bed and sang. Like flakes of flowers the words fell to the sheets. I listened to them fall and fell asleep.

The next morning the house was full of music. I was in the sun-room with Father watering our flowers. The sun was warm upon my face.

"What does she look like?" I said. "The lady in the yellow house?"

"I don't know, my dear. Not many see her face-to-face. They say that she is small, though, and that she dresses always in white."

We moved from pot to pot. He plucked the wilted petals as he went.

"Is she lonely, do you think?"

"Sometimes, I suppose. We all are lonely sometimes. But she has her sister to keep her company, and like us she has her flowers. And they say that she writes poetry."

"What is poetry?" I asked.

He laid the wilted petals in his palm. "Listen to Mother play. She practices and practices a piece, and sometimes a magic happens and it seems the music starts to breathe. It sends a shiver through you. You can't explain it, really; it's a mystery. Well, when words do that, we call it poetry."

Sunset turned the windows in the yellow house to gold. Soon the night would come. I lined the lily bulbs in a row along the sill. They looked dull and dead, like the bluebells that the letter brought. But Father says they have a hidden life, and if we plant them in the ground in spring, the sun and rain will make them start to grow.

Downstairs, Mother played. Tomorrow she would visit the yellow house. I asked her and she said that I might go. It made me feel afraid.

Perhaps the lady in the yellow house is also afraid, I thought. That is why she hides herself. That is why she runs when strangers call. But why—you cannot say. Maybe people are a mystery, too, sometimes.

The next morning the snow had begun to melt from the garden. A robin settled on the sudden grass. It was a sign of spring. Across the street the hedge had lost its veil. A shade rose in the window of the upper room.

I saw the gift of bluebells on the sill. What gift could I bring to the yellow house?

Mother wore her new silk dress, the one that whispered when she walked. The dress I wore was white, like the disappearing snow. The pockets bulged with something I had brought. Father stood and watched us from the door.

Our feet rang on the wooden walk. The road was full of mud and mirrors where the sky peeked at itself. The yellow house slipped down behind the hedge as we came near.

"Come in," said the woman who answered the door. "Oh, we have a little one, I see. Emily will be pleased."

She walked us down a whispering hall, past a door, a spill of stairs, into a parlor at the rear.

The curtains were drawn. The room was stiff and dim. The piano stood against the wall. A pot of hyacinths bloomed upon a table. The air was dizzy with their purple smell. I turned and saw a rush of white escaping up the stairs.

"Please make yourselves at home," the woman said. "It was so good of you to come. My sister is unwell today and fears she cannot join you. But she will hear you when you play." She showed me to a chair and left the room.

Mother settled at the stool. Her fingers seemed to tremble on the keys as she began to play. The music drifted through the darkened room. My hands went to my pockets and hid themselves away.

When Mother stopped she turned to me. A sound of clapping rippled down the stairs, and then a small voice like a little girl's.

"Dear friend, you put the robin's song to shame. Play more. Already I can feel the spring."

Now when the music started I crept quietly from the room. I tiptoed to the bottom of the stairs. My heart beat quickly as a little bird's. I started slowly up. At the winding of the stairs I stopped.

There at the top sat a woman all in white. At first she did not see me. She sat on a tiny chair; a stub of pencil flashed across a paper on her lap. Then she looked up.

"You little rascal, you," she said. "Come here."

I stood beside her. Our dresses both were snow. I looked down at the paper in her lap.

"Is that poetry?" I asked.

"No, you are poetry. This only tries to be." Her voice was light and brittle, like the bluebells on the windowsill.

"I brought you some spring," I said. From the pockets of my dress I took two lily bulbs and laid them in her lap. "If you plant them they will turn to lilies."

"How lovely," she said. "But surely I must give you something too." Her pencil dashed across the paper on her knee, as Mother's fingers flashed across the keys. She folded it and handed it to me.

"Here," she said. "Hide this away, as I will hide your gift to me. Perhaps in time they both will bloom."

I sat upon the parlor chair. Still the music played—but now I felt it breathe. My hand felt in my pocket. I thought of sunlight dancing on the sun-room floor, of Father plucking petals, and of poetry.

When Mother finished, she turned to me and smiled. The woman came in with a silver tray. There was a glass of sherry and a piece of gingerbread.

"How beautifully you play," she said. "We are most grateful you could come."

She sat with us while Mother sipped the sherry and I ate the gingerbread. And then it was time to go. The little bit of sherry left in the glass was the color of Emily's eyes.

Soon the spring came, and one day Father helped me plant the lily bulbs below my room.

"I was sure there were more," he said. I thought of Emily in her garden behind the high hedge, hiding my gift below the ground.

Soon the sun and rain would make them start to grow. The leaves would rise up from the soil, and then the lilies, all in white, would bloom. This, too, is a mystery.

So many, many things are Mystery.

Who has not found the Heaven—below—
Will fail of it above—
For Angels rent the House next ours,
Wherever we remove—

        Lovingly,

        Emily—

Afterword

Emily Dickinson was born in the town of Amherst, Massachusetts, in 1830. She died there in 1886. Her life, on the surface, was uneventful. She never married, never moved from home. As time went on she became increasingly reclusive, so that for the last twenty-five years of her life she did not venture beyond the bounds of her father's property.

Yet she invested the small world in which she lived with wonder. She was a skilled gardener and a keen observer of nature. Throughout her life she wrote poetry, often on scraps of paper—whatever was at hand. Upon her death, her sister discovered in the cherry-wood bureau in her room a cache of nearly 1,800 poems.

Though she was very timid of strangers, Emily was always a friend to children. Neighbor children would sometimes come around to the kitchen to talk with her while she worked. They spoke of her ready smile, her dancing eyes. She would often lower gifts of gingerbread to them from her second-floor window in a basket on a string.

In writing this book, I went to Amherst to visit the house where she lived. I sat in the parlor with the piano, visited the room where she wrote. I stood beneath her window and she lowered this story to me.

—Michael Bedard

ABOUT THE AUTHOR

MICHAEL BEDARD has written several books for children, including the biography *William Blake: The Gates of Paradise*. He has also written novels for older children, the most recent of which is *Stained Glass*. Michael Bedard's extensive research while he was writing *Emily* took him to Emily Dickinson's home in Amherst. He lives in Toronto, Canada, with his family.

ABOUT THE ILLUSTRATOR

BARBARA COONEY wrote and illustrated many books for children over her long career. *Miss Rumphius*, which she wrote and illustrated, received the American Book Award. *Ox-Cart Man*, by Donald Hall, and *Chanticleer and the Fox*, which she both retold and illustrated, won Caldecott Medals. Barbara Cooney also traveled to Amherst to do research and to sketch the Dickinson Homestead and the Kingman home across the street.

ABOUT THE BOOK

The illustrations for this book were painted on China silk mounted on illustration board and covered in two coats of gesso. Liquitex acrylic paints, Prismacolor, and Derwent colored pencils and pastels were used. The book is set in 16-point ITC Goudy Old Style. The typography is by Lynn Braswell.